WITHDRAWN
DAUPHIN COUNTY LIBRARY SYSTEM

THE QUEEN WITH BEES IN HER HAIR

For Peggy and Kim

Copyright © 1993 by Cheryl Harness
All rights reserved, including the right to reproduce
this book or portions thereof in any form.

First edition
Published by Henry Holt and Company, Inc.,
115 West 18th Street, New York, New York 10011.
Published simultaneously in Canada by Fitzhenry & Whiteside Ltd.,
91 Granton Drive, Richmond Hill, Ontario L4B 2N5.

Library of Congress Cataloging-in-Publication Data
Harness, Cheryl.
The queen with bees in her hair / Cheryl Harness.
Summary: Relates how a silly queen and a hermit king come
to join their separate kingdoms into one.
ISBN 0-8050-1715-1   [1. Fairy tales.]   I. Title.
PZ8.H235Qu   1993   [E]—dc20   92-14409

Printed in the United States of America
on acid-free paper.∞

1 3 5 7 9 10 8 6 4 2

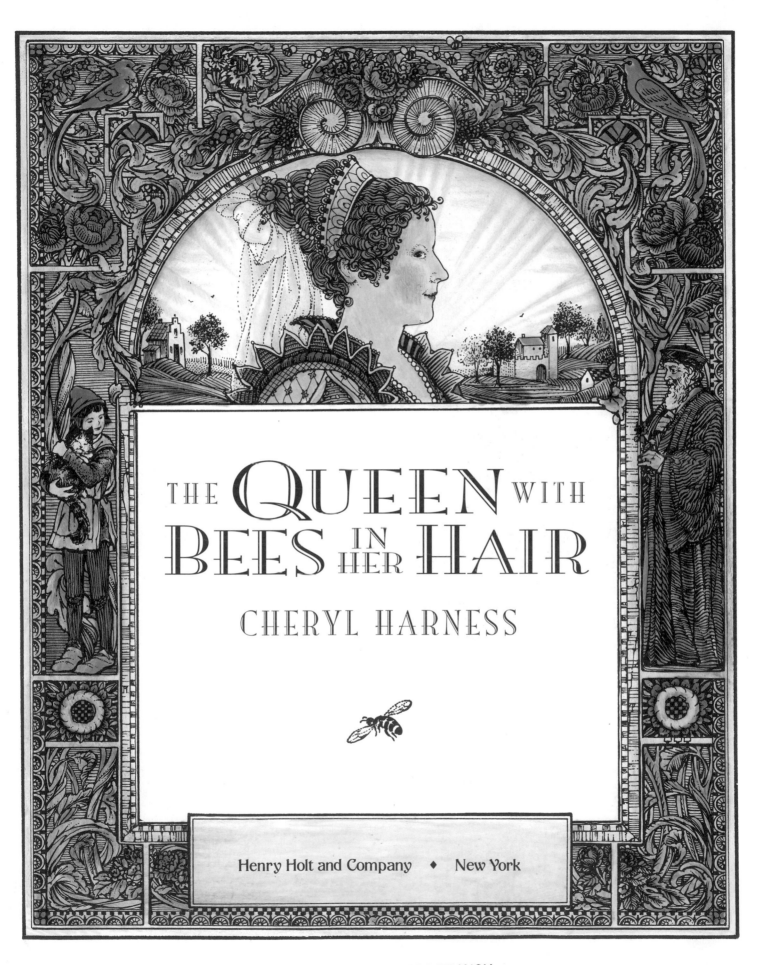

THE QUEEN WITH BEES IN HER HAIR

CHERYL HARNESS

Henry Holt and Company ◆ New York

ELIZABETHVILLE AREA BRANCH
DAUPHIN COUNTY LIBRARY SYSTEM

Once there were two kingdoms side by side. For no good reason that anyone could remember, a wall separated them, and the people seldom visited back and forth.

One kingdom was ruled by the Hermit King Harry. He had never been seen by his people, for he never left his castle. The other was ruled by Queen Ruby. Her subjects saw her when she took her carriage rides on Saturdays.

Most days, Queen Ruby sat in her garden,
brushing her long red hair. "My country is so lucky
to have such a pretty queen," she often thought.
One beautiful spring morning, while gazing at the
roses in her garden, the Queen had an idea. She
called for her ladies-in-waiting.

"Pick forty of the finest roses and fasten them in my hair," she told them. "My subjects will be delighted! They must be so weary of seeing me in an ordinary crown."

When the Queen's ladies had accomplished this feat, they clapped their hands at the effect.

Then Queen Ruby went for her carriage ride through the streets of her kingdom. But before the white horses had taken twenty steps across the cobblestones, a bee buzzed past the Queen's ear and lit upon one of the roses in her hair. Then came all the bee's friends and relatives. The buzzing was frightful. Queen Ruby swatted at them with her small white hands.

"Shoo! Go away!" she cried.

The crowds hushed. The bees stung the tip of the Queen's nose and one of her delicate white fingers.

She ordered the carriage back to the palace and shouted for her guards. "Capture every dreadful bee in my kingdom!" she stormed. "Take them all across the border. I will not be attacked in this manner!"

The weeping Queen took to her bedchamber. Her hair was mussed and her nose and finger were swelling up red.

When it was dark, the Queen's guards released black sacks of bees over the wall between the kingdoms.

The·bees·made·new·homes·for·themselves·in·the·meadows·of·King Harry's land.

The following Saturday, Queen Ruby was feeling much better. She called for her ladies to pick the finest of the crimson trumpet flowers and fasten them about her head.

"What a beautifully royal effect!" she exclaimed, admiring herself in the mirror. "And what a delightful red in the little trumpets!"

The Queen began her carriage ride, and the people cheered. But before the carriage had entered the marketplace, at least seventeen hummingbirds were flying around the Queen's head. They dipped their slender beaks in the crimson trumpets as the Queen tried to shoo them away in a dignified manner.

"Be gone, I say!"

Their humming and fluttering were so alarming that the outraged Queen ordered the carriage turned back.

"Guards! Guards!" she cried. "Capture every last hummingbird in my kingdom! Toss them over the border. Let Harry's people deal with them. I've no patience with the little beasts!"

The next Saturday morning, the Queen sat in her sunny garden eating breakfast.

"What a lovely day," she said with a happy sigh as she ate her blackberries and cream. "I should surpass even myself on such a day." The Queen had another idea.

An hour later, the ladies-in-waiting had dressed the Queen's hair in a glorious wreath of blackberries and green leaves.

"Oh, this is by far the most regal and beautiful effect I have ever achieved! My subjects will be thrilled!"

Before the Queen's retinue had passed the courtyard gates, songbirds of every kind began pecking at the Queen's head. They ate all the blackberries and got tangled in her red hair.

The people's cheering turned to poorly hidden gasps and giggles at the remarkable sight.

"I demand that you catch every songbird in the kingdom!" the angry Queen shouted. "And mind you get their little eggs too! Let Harry's people be pecked and flapped to distraction. I will not tolerate these attacks on my person!"

The · guards · climbed · up · in · the · trees ·
with · baskets · and · birdcages ·

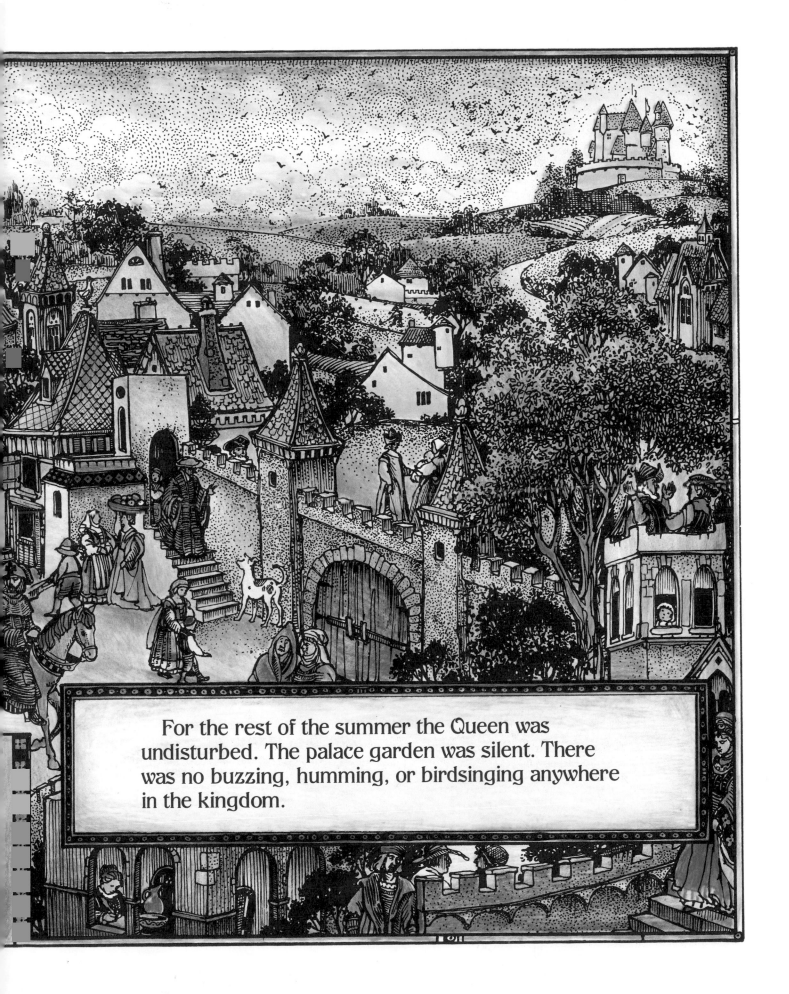

For the rest of the summer the Queen was undisturbed. The palace garden was silent. There was no buzzing, humming, or birdsinging anywhere in the kingdom.

In the autumn, the Queen became fancier as her people became more somber. When she went out in her carriage, her dutiful subjects applauded her beauty, but their cheers were halfhearted. Queen Ruby wore garlands of grapes and mums and maple leaves. In the winter, she wore pinecones, holly, and summer flowers carefully dried.

"Soon we'll have delightful fresh flowers," said the Queen. "It will be spring!" Her ladies-in-waiting looked doubtfully at the snowy courtyard.

Spring came, but without a single flower.

"The hives are empty of honey," said the nervous Prime Minister. "Without bees to carry pollen, we'll have neither fruit nor flowers. And were there to be any crops in the fields, insects would eat them since there are no birds to eat the bugs. The land will suffer, Your Majesty."

Queen Ruby had to admit that she missed the birds singing in her garden.

"I didn't really mind those nasty bees when they stayed where they belonged," she said with a sigh. Then she began to frown.

"My subjects are unhappy," she thought. "Soon they will be hungry. They might become angry. There might even be a revolution!"

She had read of such things happening.

"Even the most beautiful queen would fare poorly in a revolution!" Queen Ruby thought with a shudder. She ran to her balcony and called for her guards.

"Go to King Harry's land," she shouted, "and fetch back our birds and bees! And be quick about it!"

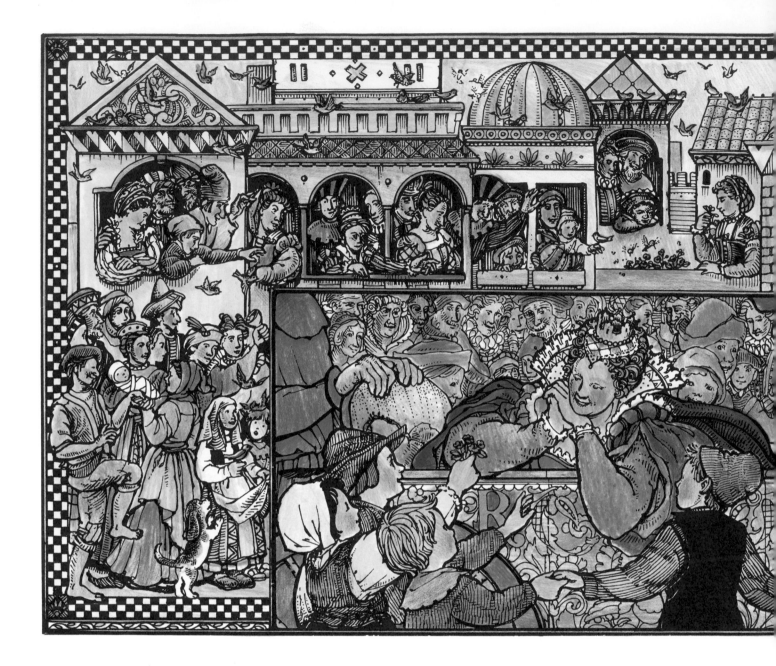

Before the sun set twice, Ruby's kingdom was full of buzzing, humming, and birdsong. There was a celebration throughout the land. Queen Ruby, wearing a sensible crown, rode in her carriage on a Thursday, breaking all tradition. The Queen glanced warily at the sky, then smiled a relieved smile at her cheering subjects.

　　As the royal white horses drew the carriage
through the streets, the Queen and the people
smiled and waved at each other.
　　"I never knew what nice people my subjects
are!" said Queen Ruby to her footman. Then she
had a wonderful idea.
　　"Everybody come to the palace tonight! We will
have a party to celebrate spring!"

That evening, at the height of the feasting and dancing, a coach bearing the crest of Hermit King Harry was driven to the front door of Queen Ruby's palace. In the lamplight and shadows were all of his wondering, whispering subjects, who had followed along to see where the King was going and what he looked like.

When the guard came to the door, King Harry shyly poked his head out the coach's window. He had shiny dark eyes and soft brown whiskers.

He cleared his throat and said, "Excuse me, but I must meet your generous Queen. My ministers tell me that our crops were abundant and our gardens have bloomed as never before. I must thank Ruby for the loan of your bees and birds."

Everyone hushed and stared as the King was taken to Queen Ruby. Harry felt very uncomfortable. He thought, "I'm a king, after all; I must say something!"

"Why, you are as beautiful as you are bountiful," said the King. "It was splendid of you, Queen Ruby, to send your birds and bees over," he continued nervously. "How ever did you think of it?"

The guards rolled their eyes toward the ceiling as the ladies-in-waiting smiled behind their fans. Before the blushing Queen could reply, the Prime Minister whispered in her ear.

"Won't you join me on the balcony?" Ruby asked the King. "The people are waiting to see us."

"My people have never seen me before," King Harry confessed shyly.

"Oh Harry, I wouldn't worry," Queen Ruby replied. "Before today, I'd never really seen my people!"

With that, the King and Queen went
out on the balcony to greet their subjects.

As time went on, the historic spring turned to summer, and soon enough no one paid any attention to the wall between the kingdoms. King Harry, Queen Ruby, and all the people, bees, and birds lived in harmony forever after.

JUN 2 2 1993

WITHDRAWN
DAUPHIN COUNTY LIBRARY SYSTEM

DATE DUE		
SEP 25 1998		
OCT 2 4 1998		
DEC 2 9 1998		
APR 1 2 1999		
GAYLORD		PRINTED IN U.S.A.